This book belongs to:

....

....

For my Mum and Dad

A TEMPLAR BOOK

First published in the UK in 2022 by Templar Books,
an imprint of Bonnier Books UK
4th Floor, Victoria House,
Bloomsbury Square, London WC1B 4DA
Owned by Bonnier Books
Sveavägen 56, Stockholm, Sweden
www.bonnierbooks.co.uk

Text and illustration copyright © 2022 by Bethany Christou
Design copyright © 2022 by Templar Books

1 3 5 7 9 10 8 6 4 2

ISBN 978-1-80078-160-3 (Paperback)

This book was typeset in Trocchi
The illustrations were created with gouache paint,
coloured pencils, acrylic paint, pastels and digital painting

Edited by Samuel Fern and Amelia Warren
Designed by Ted Jennings
Production by Ella Holden

Printed in China

FSC
www.fsc.org

MIX
Paper from
responsible sources
FSC® C104723

I'M MORE THAN A SHEEP

Bethany Christou

templar
books

Being a sheep meant eating the same food as everyone else,

running in the same direction as eveyone else,

and sometimes having
her coat removed
(like everyone else).

How
embarrassing.

Mildred *tried* to stand
out from the crowd...

I'm now the
most fashionable
sheep.

... but she was never different for long.

"*Looking* different isn't enough," thought Mildred.
"They'll all just copy me."

"I need to do something special. Something no other sheep can do."

"I need to be more like... "

"I am magnificent, aren't I?" said the horse. "And I'm the fastest runner around."

"Perhaps I could be as fast as a horse!" thought Mildred.

She landed on the
other side of the fence with a...

Splat!

Here, Mildred found another
magnificent creature.

"What are you?"
she asked.

"We are chickens. And we lay the most beautiful eggs!"

"I'm going to be the first sheep to lay an egg," decided Mildred.

Mildred tried her hardest.

But what she laid was definitely NOT an egg.

Mildred tried many things.

She tried learning how to dig,

how to swim,

how to be flexible,

and how to fly.

Every one of these skills would have made Mildred stand out from her flock. But she wasn't good at *any* of them.

Just when she was about to give up, Mildred saw the most **_magnificent_** creature of them all.

"How do I be more like you?" asked Mildred.

Ms Wolf turned and said, "Why, don't you know?
We wolves love dinner parties. I'm hosting
one tonight, and I'd *love* to have you."

A sheep, dining with wolves!
That would make Mildred
special indeed.

"Where are the other guests?" asked Mildred,
as they arrived at Ms Wolf's house.

"Oh, they'll be here later," answered Ms Wolf.
"Put this parsley behind your ear. It's very fashionable."

"What do wolves eat?" asked Mildred.

"Dinner will be a surprise," replied Ms Wolf.
"Now rub this butter... I mean moisturiser... all over you.
It will make you silky smooth, just like me."

"What's this bubbling pot for?" asked Mildred.
"That's the jacuzzi," said Ms Wolf.
"Wolves always have a nice warm dip before a big meal."

"And as my guest, I *insist* you go first."

MEALS FOR WOLVES

LAMB RECIPES

COOK SHEEP STEW

"I... I don't think I want to be like you anymore," said Mildred.

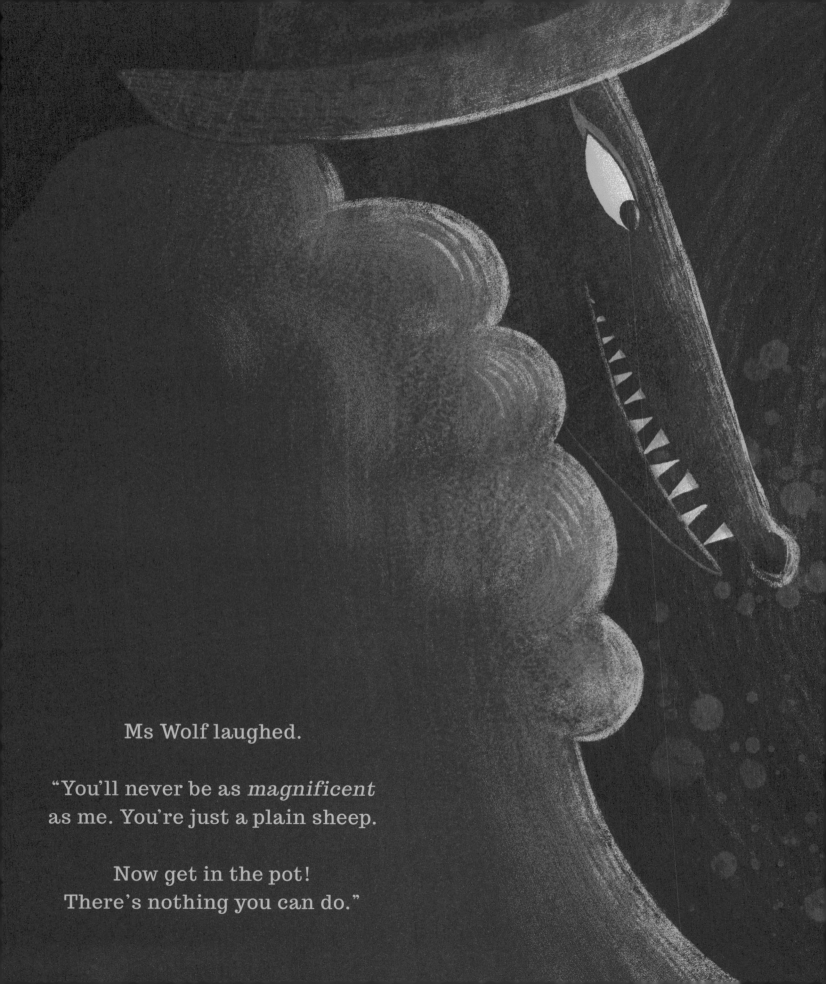

Ms Wolf laughed.

"You'll never be as *magnificent*
as me. You're just a plain sheep.

Now get in the pot!
There's nothing you can do."

"Well," said Mildred.
"THERE IS ONE THING I CAN DO!"

And she let out an enormous...

BAAAAAA

Ms Wolf fell backwards into the pot.

"YOWWWWW!" she cried. "What's going on?"

"Why, don't you know?" said Mildred.
"Where one sheep goes, the rest will follow."

For the first time, being part of a flock
seemed like a wonderful thing.

BAAAAA

"Let's go home," said Mildred, as she led the way.

Although her flock grew and grew,
there could only ever be one Mildred...

More beautiful books from Bethany Christou...

Slow
Samson

Bethany Christou

Party
this way →

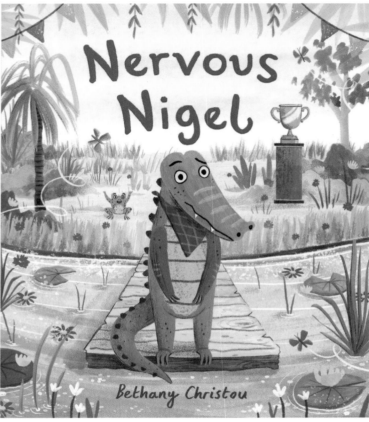

Nervous
Nigel

Bethany Christou